THE CLONE WARS™

THE GALACTIC PHOTOBOOK

Adapted by Zachary Rau

Based on the movie *Star Wars: The Clone Wars*

Grosset & Dunlap · LucasBooks

GROSSET & DUNLAP

Published by the Penguin Group

Penguin Group (USA) Inc., 375 Hudson Street, New York, New York 10014, USA

Penguin Group (Canada), 90 Eglinton Avenue East, Suite 700, Toronto, Ontario M4P 2Y3, Canada (a division of Pearson Penguin Canada Inc.)

Penguin Books Ltd., 80 Strand, London WC2R 0RL, England

Penguin Group Ireland, 25 St. Stephen's Green, Dublin 2, Ireland (a division of Penguin Books Ltd.)

Penguin Group (Australia), 250 Camberwell Road, Camberwell, Victoria 3124, Australia (a division of Pearson Australia Group Pty. Ltd.)

Penguin Books India Pvt. Ltd., 11 Community Centre, Panchsheel Park, New Delhi—110 017, India

Penguin Group (NZ), 67 Apollo Drive, Rosedale, North Shore 0632, New Zealand (a division of Pearson New Zealand Ltd.)

Penguin Books (South Africa) (Pty.) Ltd., 24 Sturdee Avenue, Rosebank, Johannesburg 2196, South Africa

Penguin Books Ltd., Registered Offices:

80 Strand, London WC2R 0RL, England

The publisher does not have any control over and does not assume any responsibility for author or third-party websites or their content.

Library of Congress Cataloging-in-Publication Data is available.

ISBN: 978-0-448-44996-8   10 9 8 7 6 5 4 3 2 1

A long time ago, in a galaxy far, far away....

The Republic is at war! Supreme Chancellor Palpatine has committed thousands of troops to the war against Count Dooku's Separatist Alliance. As planets choose sides, the galaxy is divided and only the valiant efforts of Republic clone troopers and their Jedi generals hold the fracturing Republic from tearing apart.

Anakin Skywalker and Obi-Wan Kenobi have scored a rare victory for the Republic on the planet Christophsis. A new Padawan learner arrives in time to aid the Jedi, but she's not to study under Obi-Wan as expected, but under Anakin, who swore he'd never take an apprentice.

As war spreads chaos across the galaxy, crime lord Jabba the Hutt's son is kidnapped. In order to gain safe passage through the Hutt's systems, the Jedi have agreed to find and rescue Jabba's son.

Obi-Wan Kenobi

JEDI

The noble Jedi Master Obi-Wan Kenobi is a high-ranking general in the clone army. Disciplined and courageous, Obi-Wan fights to preserve the Republic from the evil plans of the Separatists. Obi-Wan now finds endless delight in watching his one-time student, Anakin Skywalker, struggle with a strong-willed learner of his own.

On Tatooine, Obi-Wan concludes his meeting with the feared Jabba the Hutt . . .

ALL RIGHT ANAKIN, HERE'S THE STORY.

. . . and immediately contacts Anakin and his new Padawan, Ahsoka Tano, to fill them in on the details of Rotta the Huttlet's kidnapping.

JABBA HAS GIVEN US ONLY ONE PLANETARY ROTATION TO GET HIS SON BACK HOME TO TATOOINE SAFE AND SOUND.

IT WON'T TAKE US THAT LONG, MASTER.

WE HAVE NO IDEA WHO IS HOLDING JABBA'S SON. WHEN I'VE FINISHED NEGOTIATIONS WITH HIM, I WILL JOIN YOU.

Rotta
the Huttlet

Rotta, the son of Jabba the Hutt, is only a fraction of the size he will eventually grow to be. He may be cute now, but he is heir to one of the most powerful crime organizations in the galaxy.

Anakin and Ahsoka's investigation leads them to planet Teth . . .

I SENSE OUR KIDNAPPED HUTT IS IN HERE.

. . . where they find Rotta the Huttlet in a dungeon.

WAAAAAAH!

Rotta is sick, crying, and misses his father.

HE'S JUST A BABY. THIS WILL MAKE OUR JOB A LOT EASIER. HE'S SO CUTE!

WAAAAH!

Count Dooku

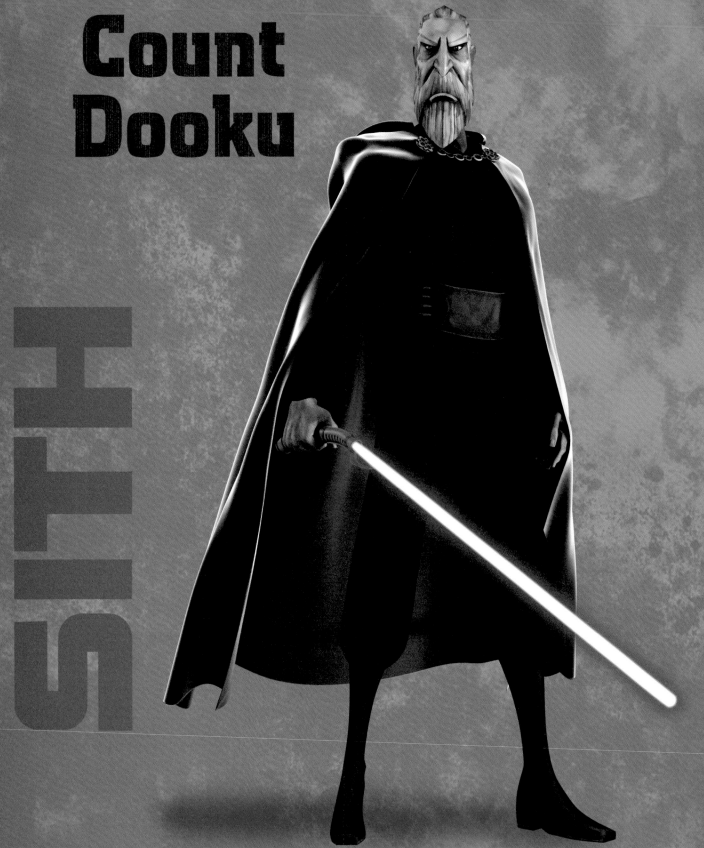

Once a Jedi Master, Count Dooku is the leader and general of the Separatists. His charismatic ways have swayed many planets to the Separatist cause. He has fully embraced the ancient teachings of the Sith and is now known as Darth Tyranus. He uses his knowledge of the Jedi Order to wreak havoc across the galaxy and cause confusion within the Jedi Council.

Battle Droid, Super Battle Droid, and Droideka

Battle droids, super battle droids, and droidekas comprise the majority of Count Dooku's Separatist Army. While not living creatures, some of these robots develop their own eccentric personalities.

R2-D2

DROID

Artoo-Detoo is a fearless, quick-thinking, and dedicated astromech droid. He is a tireless worker, a sympathetic listener, and always ready for action when the chips are down.

Dooku's assassin, Asajj Ventress, finds the Jedi as they try to rescue Rotta.

MASTER SKYWALKER, I'VE BEEN SO LOOKING FORWARD TO ANOTHER ENCOUNTER WITH YOU. I SEE YOU'VE FOUND YOURSELF A NEW PET.

I'M NO PET!

CAREFUL, SHE BITES!

JUST GIVE ME THE HUTT, SKYWALKER! I WILL FINISH YOU FIRST, SO YOU WON'T HAVE TO WATCH YOUR SILLY YOUNGLING DIE.

BEE BOO BOOP!

Secretly, Artoo-Detoo glides over to one of the castle's electronic instrument panels that controls the grate that everyone is standing on.

The grate opens, sending the Jedi, Ventress, and her battle droids plummeting to unknown levels below.

The little droid even knocks the last of the battle droids over the edge.

AAAAAAAAAH!

WHAM!

Clone Trooper

CLONE

Bred and trained on the oceanic outlying planet Kamino, the unflinchingly loyal clone troopers are born to serve the Republic. Despite sharing identical genes, a clone trooper often fosters a greater sense of identity by giving himself a name, a stylized haircut, or even the occasional tattoo. While a clone's role may not seem an enviable one, the hardships of battle create an unparalleled bond between the soldiers.

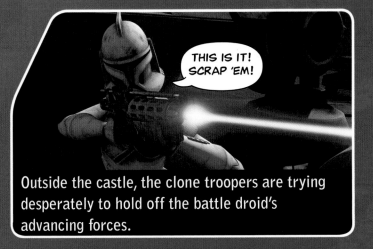

Outside the castle, the clone troopers are trying desperately to hold off the battle droid's advancing forces.

No matter how hard they fight, there are just too many battle droids.

SURRENDER, REPUBLIC DOGS!

WE'VE GOT YOU OUTNUMBERED!

Eventually, the clone troopers are surrounded.

Suddenly, Obi-Wan arrives with much needed reinforcements.

VZZZZZKT

KA-BOOM!

WHERE'S SKYWALKER?

BEST GUESS SAYS HE'S STILL IN THE CASTLE, SIR.

KEEP THE DROIDS OCCUPIED. I'LL GO FIND HIM.

Ahsoka Tano

Jedi Moral Code #2:
The wise Jedi does not
trust appearances.

A teenage Togruta, Ahsoka, is eager to prove herself as a worthy Padawan to her bold Master, Anakin Skywalker. Ahsoka complements Anakin's aggressive tendencies with a disarming innocence and wit. She can wield a lightsaber and pilot a spacecraft with equal talent. Straddling the chasm between Anakin's impulsiveness and Obi-Wan's cautious nature, Ahsoka promises to become a worthy Jedi . . . if she survives the war.

Having just escaped from the assassin Ventress, Anakin and Ahsoka find a run-down spice freighter on an empty landing platform near the castle.

The Jedi prepare to take off and head toward Jabba's palace on Tatooine . . .

. . . but the engines fail to ignite.

NOW LET'S GET STINKY OUTTA HERE. UH, IF WE CAN!

BUURP

ARTOO, SEE IF YOU CAN SPARK THE IGNITION COUPLERS.

DEE BOO BEEP

Once again, Artoo-Detoo saves the day.

The engines roar to life and the spice freighter *Twilight* takes off.

Clone Captain Rex

CLONE

Anakin's second-in-command, Captain Rex, is a freethinking and aggressive soldier. Gruff, no-nonsense, and tough as nails, Rex voices his professional opinion to even the highest-ranking Jedi. In command of the famed 501st Legion of clone troopers, Rex and his men are assigned to patrol the most lawless and dangerous sectors of the galaxy, the feared Outer Rim.

SEPARATIST

Asajj
Ventress

Count Dooku's most trusted assassin, Asajj
Ventress, is a lithe beauty possessing both serpentine
grace and lethality. Though she's not officially a Sith
apprentice, Ventress has clearly been well-trained in the arts
of lightsaber dueling and Force manipulation. If Dooku's Master, the
terrifying Darth Sidious, ever finds out about Ventress's education,
the consequences will be dire for both teacher and student.

Yoda

JEDI

At nearly nine hundred years old, Yoda is without peer in his knowledge of the Force. He wields his lightsaber with blinding speed and uses his agility to render himself nearly invulnerable. In an attempt to teach Anakin responsibility, Yoda has given his newest general a Padawan learner named Ahsoka, but Yoda often wonders if his decision to pair the volatile duo has simply created twice the trouble for the Jedi Council.

Ziro the Hutt

Another member of the Hutt clan, Ziro, is not as large as his nephew Jabba, but his hunger for power is just as great. Based on Coruscant, he will do anything to increase his position in the clan.

YOUR MAJESTY, YOU HAVE AN IMPORTANT VISITOR.

GREETINGS, ZIRO! I AM SENATOR AMIDALA OF THE GALACTIC SENATE. I KNOW THAT YOU ARE THE UNCLE OF JABBA THE HUTT OF TATOOINE.

I HAVE COME HERE TO ASK A FAVOR OF YOU. I WAS HOPING YOU AND I COULD RESOLVE THIS DISPUTE AND BROKER A TREATY BETWEEN THE REPUBLIC AND THE GREAT CLAN OF THE HUTTS!

Elsewhere, Senator Padmé Amidala is sent to seek a treaty with the lone member of the Hutt clan on Coruscant.

A TREATY! A TREATY! A TREATY IS IMPOSSIBLE! MY NEPHEW HAS BEEN KIDNAPPED BY YOUR REPUBLIC JEDI SCUM!

BUT, SIR, THERE HAS BEEN A MISUNDERSTANDING.

NO! NO MORE DISCUSSIONS. ESCORT HER OUT!

As Senator Amidala is escorted out of Ziro's palace, she becomes convinced that she needs to talk to Ziro again and gives her guard the slip.

She returns to the throne room to find Ziro communicating with a sinister figure.

YOUR PLOT IS COMING APART, COUNT DOOKU! A SENATOR FROM THE REPUBLIC WAS HERE! WHAT IF SHE FINDS OUT I HELPED YOU KIDNAP JABBA'S SON?!

COUNT DOOKU! SO, THE POISONOUS TRAITOR REARS HIS UGLY HEAD ONCE AGAIN!

I'M EQUALLY DELIGHTED TO REMAKE YOUR ACQUAINTANCE, SENATOR . . . AMIDALA, ISN'T IT?

The Senator is not as quiet as she hoped and is noticed by the two conspirators.

ANAKIN SKYWALKER

JEDI

Brash, young Jedi Knight Anakin Skywalker leads the clone armies of the Republic into battle against the Separatist forces during the galaxy-wide tumult of the Clone Wars. Together with his Padawan, Ahsoka, Anakin uses his superior Force abilities to cunningly escape Separatist traps, maneuver through dangerous space battles, and boldly confront his own fateful destiny.

Padmé Amidala

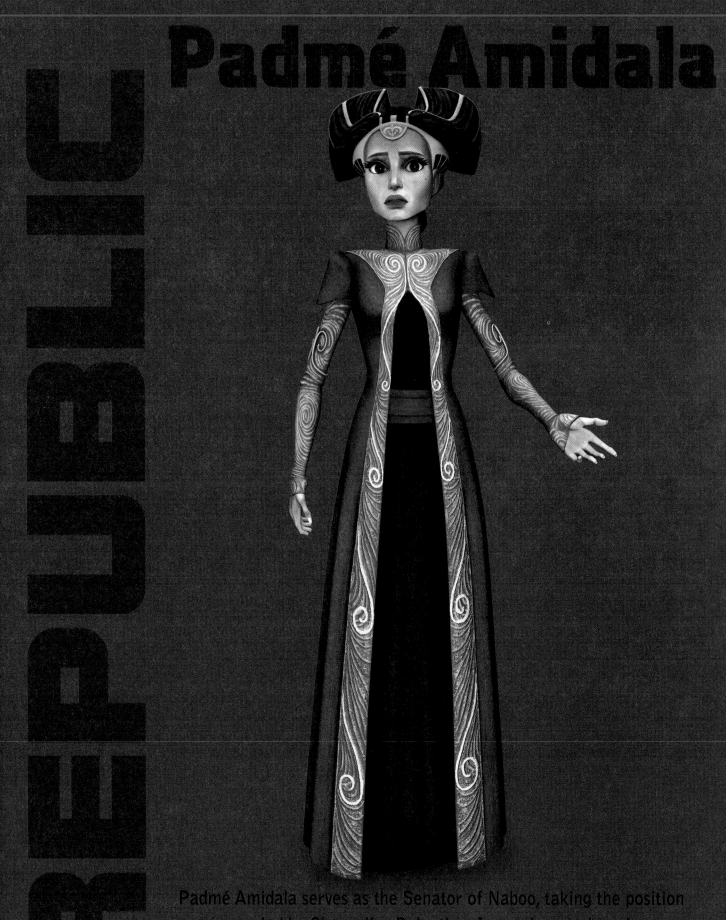

Padmé Amidala serves as the Senator of Naboo, taking the position once occupied by Chancellor Palpatine. In a galaxy undergoing tumultuous changes, her outspoken nature has shone as a beacon of reason and rationality in an increasingly fragmented senate.

Jabba the Hutt

A loathsome slug of a gangster, Jabba the Hutt, is the kingpin of crime in the Outer Rim Territories.

Chancellor Palpatine

Once elected to power, Chancellor Palpatine set his plans in motion. Atop his perch on Coruscant, he uses the skills he learned as Darth Sidious to bring down the Republic and take control of the entire galaxy. Few know his true identity, but Palpatine works his evil from the shadows.